Brooklyn Park Elem.

52074760

I Love My Buzzard

A Richard Jackson Book

I Love My

story by Tres Seymour

Orchard Books New York

Buzzard

with illustrations by S. D. Schindler

Orchard Books
95 Madison Avenue, New York, NY 10016

Manufactured in the United States of America.
Printed by Barton Press, Inc. Bound by Horowitz/Rae.
Typography by Duke & Company.
Book design by Maria Demopoulos.

The text of this book is set in 22-point ITC Garamond
Book Condensed. The illustrations are colored pencil
reproduced in full color.

10 9 8 7 6 5 4 3 2 1

Library of Congress Cataloging-in-Publication Data
Seymour, Tres. I love my buzzard / story by
Tres Seymour ; illustrated by S. D. Schindler. p.   cm.
"A Richard Jackson book."
Summary: A child's beloved pets; including a warthog,
bat, and squid; become less important when they
drive Mother away.
ISBN 0-531-06819-6.   ISBN 0-531-08669-0 (lib. bdg.)
[1. Pets—Fiction.   2. Mother and child—Fiction.
3. Stories in rhyme.]   I. Schindler, S. D., ill.   II. Title.
PZ8.3.S496Iam   1994   [E]—dc20   93- 4877

I love my buzzard and my buzzard loves me.
I feed him five fish heads a day.

He likes me to polish the top of his head.
My mom does not wish him to stay.

I love my warthog and my warthog loves me.
He blows his round nose on my sleeve.

He borrows my toothpaste, my brush, and my floss.
My mom has asked him to leave.

I love my bat and my bat loves me.
He hovers six feet off the floor.

He makes a good hat
when he spreads out his wings.
My mom will not open the door.

I love my squid and my squid loves me.
I give him long baths in the sink.
He teaches me how to tie knots with his toes.
He gives Mom the willies, I think.

I love my iguana and my iguana loves me.
I comb the green spines on his back.

He likes to lick people
    just under their knees.
My mom has gone upstairs to pack.

I love my slugs and my slugs love me.
They like to sleep in a big jar,
Though they're often mistaken for jelly instead.
My mom just drove off in the car.

I love my buzzard, my warthog, and bat.
My squid is a huggable dear.
I prize my iguana and cherish my slugs.
But I wish that my mother were here.

So I'll send them away to find a new home
With a week's worth of food in a sack.

I'll wait by the door, and if I am lucky
Then maybe—

My mom will come back.